THE LAST TOWER

THE LAST TOWER

BRIAN OXLEY

OXVISION
books
thelasttower.com

AUTHOR
Brian Oxley

GENERAL EDITOR
Beckie Oxley

ILLUSTRATORS
Tim Ladwig
Chris Koelle (Epilogue)

BOOK DESIGN & LAYOUT
Erik Peterson

BOOK CO-SPONSOR
Chris Oxley

TYPEFACES
Ideal Sans, FF Scala

WITH SPECIAL THANKS TO:

BETTY OXLEY
for encouraging me in my writing of this book

BILL POLLARD
for listening to me, and giving me feedback
as the book progressed

GREG BANDY
for advising me on the book concept and
helping with the writing

JAMES BELL
for editing early story concepts

JOE RITCHIE
for supporting me on my journey

LON LUCIEER
for tirelessly working as the Associate Editor

MICHAEL BANNON
for excellent teachings from the book of
Ecclesiastes, from which I drew material for
the book, and helping to rewrite the text

SALLY OXLEY
for collaborating on every aspect of the book

FIRST U.S. EDITION
ISBN 978 1 938068 00 3

Printed in the USA by Spectrum Printing of Orlando, FL

Published by OxVision Books, a division of
BridgePoint International, LLC, 2135 City Gate Lane, Naperville, IL 60563

Watch the book trailer at: **www.thelasttower.com**
Find us at: **www.oxvisionbooks.com**

US $20 * JAPAN ¥1,600

TABLE OF CONTENTS

Preface   xiii

CHAPTER 1
A Sketch of the Imagination   3

CHAPTER 2
The Unraveling   17

CHAPTER 3
The Foreboding   35

CHAPTER 4
Fiat Currencies   43

CHAPTER 5
The Resource Grab   55

CHAPTER 6
Treading the Wheels   65

CHAPTER 7
Babel II   81

CHAPTER 8
The Crystal Tree   95

CHAPTER 9
The Uniqueness of Man   103

CHAPTER 10
Bread and Circuses   117

CHAPTER 11
The Red Wave   127

Epilogue   135

TO SALLY
my wife, my friend, my love

Our hearts beat as one. Often, when I am weary
and my strength fails me, your heart beats for both of us.

At times, I have pursued greatness, yet my heart remained
in torment, for I could find none, nor could I find joy. Yet,
you – you, who never sought greatness – simply stood there,
waiting with a smile that said, "All is forgiven."

You taught me about God's love: His forgiveness of sin,
and the pain He bore for us.

When I wake early in the morning, reach out for you,
and find you not there, I am comforted in the knowledge
that you are spending time with Him.

God has blessed our lives with three wonderful daughters,
their husbands, and many grandchildren. Our hearts beat
all the stronger now, for there are so many more to love.

Together, we shall continue to pray that His love
will likewise beat in their hearts.

EVEN THOUGH WE HAD YEARS to prepare as a family, I still did not believe the nurse when she told me he was gone. My father, a former World War II Marine, fought his final battle with Alzheimer's, and that compassion-filled heart that I thought would beat forever, suddenly stopped.

My amazing father, one of my life's great treasures, who in my estimation deserved to be transported into heaven by mighty horses in a glorious chariot, with the Marine Band leading the way, loudly trumpeting his arrival, instead went quietly and in some pain. That was more his style; not the fanfare I thought he deserved.

The words of George MacDonald, a favorite Scottish novelist, describe my feelings as I joined my family in an embrace of grief: "Ah, Beloved! Let us love, let us cleave to one another, for we die!"

I began to write at my father's bedside a few weeks before he left us. His impending death thrust me into a world of reflection. Who am I in light of who he was? What have I done that is worthwhile in my life?

The constant news on various fronts in my country and around the world troubles me, and petty disagreements anger me. So now I write to better understand my purpose on this earth and to be the man my father was, so that when asked, I can guide my children and my grandchildren in a changing world, where sometimes we see hope dimly.

With my good friends, I ponder the current challenges we face in a world that trembles. We can already detect the tremors running beneath our feet. We must find solutions, setting our selfish desires aside, and totally committing to truth for the greater good.

In *The Golden Key*, a short fairy tale, George MacDonald wrote about the Old Man of the Earth who raises a huge stone from the floor of his cave. It discloses a great hole that goes straight down. "That is the way," he says to the child whom he is guiding. "But there are no stairs," the child protests. The man then replies, "You must throw yourself in. There is no other way." Likewise, we need to throw ourselves into the task of rebuilding our world. It may be a difficult and even dangerous assignment, but there is no other choice.

My father, a man of action, went to the land of Japan as a missionary, the land of the people he fought in World War II as a Marine. So distance, separation, and farewells were a way of life for us, but he always left me and my siblings with a promise: "If you ever really need me, call me, and I will come."

For years I never took him up on this promise, until one day our family found ourselves in a crisis as our middle daughter's kidneys stopped functioning. She was facing the prospect of lifelong dialysis, transplants, etc. I made the call, and my mom and dad came quickly from Japan and stayed with us through an extensive period of troubled waters – with a happy ending.

I can no longer call my father. All of you who have lost a father or a mother, you know of what I speak. And yet, we now face a dangerous, uncertain future in which, deep down inside, we yearn for our parents' protection and wisdom. But now is the time for all of us to consider our responsibilities here and help plot a course to sanity and safety for future generations.

To all who have lost a parent, to those who suffer with Alzheimer's, to those who fight against this illness with care and compassion, and to my dad, I dedicate this book.

Now the whole world had one language and a common speech. As people moved eastward they found a plain in Shinar and settled there. They said to each other, "Come, let's make bricks and bake them thoroughly." They used brick instead of stone, and tar for mortar. Then they said, "Come, let us build ourselves a city, with a tower that reaches to the heavens, so that we may make a name for ourselves; otherwise we will be scattered over the face of the whole earth." But the Lord came down to see the city and the tower the people were building. The Lord said, "If as one people speaking the same language they have begun to do this, then nothing they plan to do will be impossible for them. Come, let us go down and confuse their language so they will not understand each other." So the Lord scattered them from there over all the earth, and they stopped building the city. That is why it was called Babel – because there the Lord confused the language of the whole world.

Genesis 11:1-9

THE LAST TOWER

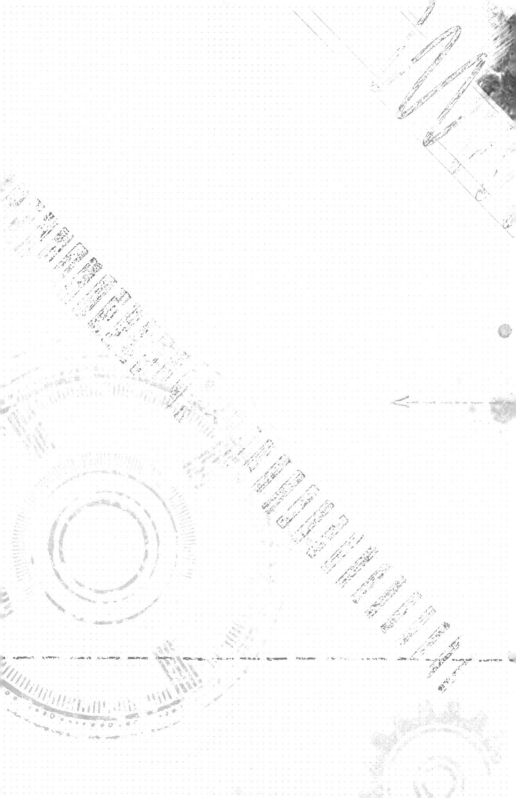

THE LAST TOWER

CHAPTER
01

A SKETCH OF
THE IMAGINATION

Our meeting place

THE LATE AFTERNOON SUN WAS partially obscured by the storm front gathering in the west. The lights shining from the window of the Star Diner cast a warm, welcoming glow that enticed the hungry to come inside and fill up on its simple but hearty fare 24 hours a day, every day, except Christmas. The diner had that warm, comfortable vibe of decades-old vinyl booths and Formica countertops where many a Blue Plate Special had been served by the crusty, but efficient waitresses common to such places. It was the gathering place for the locals because of the endless coffee cup and the fresh homemade pies, which seemed the necessary fuel for their endless discussions as they "held court" in their usual seats.

One particular group of guys came once a month. They had all attended the same prep boarding school in Tennessee, but they were anything but similar. They were a mixed bag of personalities and styles, and varying degrees of fame and wealth.

John had been the studious one. He would always arrive at the library at the same time every day; the prep scholar had been about as interesting as a nice, reliable clock. But he always had time for his friends and had played an incredibly useful role as the resident volunteer tutor.

Steve, on the other hand, had struggled with his grades and with being away from his parents. He regularly depended on John's help. It wasn't that he personally wanted good grades; he just had wanted to please his parents who were missionaries in Japan. But Steve was a clever one. He had figured out that Fs were fairly easy to draw into Bs. Every minus had a chance to be transformed into a plus, and, with a little mud, a D also could be converted into a B. Truth was, Steve basically had majored in girls and sports in high school; the girls had liked the handsome and gentle guy and would find excuses to talk to him.

Troy and Matt were the mischievous ones. They were often seen sitting together in the detention hall wearing sheepish grins, and never would one have ratted on the other. Their English teacher had been surprised one morning to find a goat tied to her chair eating the homework she had graded the previous day. Since Matt could outrun all of the other boys in PE, and could certainly outrun a goat, it was presumed that he had been the major culprit, but Troy was a bold instigator with way too many ideas for his own good.

Somehow their differences seemed to bond them even closer. Troy attended church regularly and was firm in his beliefs, but Matt had no interest in anything religious. Matt's passion was computers and he spent the hard-earned money from his first grocery store job to buy a computer.

David had been the artistic one of the group. He had loved to draw and write. His friendliness had attracted people to him, and his quirky caricatures had captured the essence of many faculty personalities. He was in fact the glue that kept the five together.

In the dorm, the friends often had gathered on Friday nights in the lounge to discuss events of the day. These discussions often encompassed a wide range of topics from sports to girls. Troy was the chief storyteller. Although sometimes they had to put pillows on his head to get him to stop talking, now and then he would tell a story that would transport their imaginations to faraway places.

Troy's parents had lived closest to the school, and often had invited the boys to visit on weekends. Steve's parents were in Japan, Matt's parents were educators in Afghanistan, and John's dad was a diplomat in Hong Kong.

David's dad was a wealthy executive in a big firm, lived in the Hamptons, and didn't have a lot of time for David. David spent more time at Troy's house on holidays than with his own parents.

All but Troy had received college degrees. Troy had stayed at home to work in his dad's cleaning business, and eventually became a commercial property window washer.

John, had always been good with numbers, and had become a fairly well-known economist and successful CPA.

David had become an architect, although some people wondered if this was the kind of drawing he had dreamed of as a child; most thought his parents had pushed him in that direction. Whenever the group got together, he always brought his pad of paper and sketched throughout the discussions.

Matt had developed his love of computers into a career as an IT consultant at a university.

Unfortunately, colleges hadn't cared for Steve's prep school "majors." After being rejected by several universities, he had gone on to junior college and had finally discovered a love of learning. He had persevered against many obstacles to graduate with a degree in engineering, much to his friends' surprise.

After drifting apart for college and early careers, the five men found themselves all living in the same city, and began meeting together to catch up and to continue the intense discussions from their dorm days together. Steve traveled internationally, so they often planned their meetings around his schedule. There was definitely a competitive male thing to their get-togethers, much like aggressive games of pick-up basketball. But even though the games got a little rough sometimes, they seemed to thrive on the sport of it all and kept getting together to "play ball."

Their wives often wondered how they stayed friends after some of the heated arguments, but the bonds forged in boarding school seemed to hang tough.

Matt, Troy, and John were already sitting in their favorite booth in the back corner when the bell above the diner door signaled another patron had been drawn in by the promise of a good meal. David blew in, his longish hair damp from the short run from his car, his ever-present portfolio shielded under his arm. John and Troy looked up, as he made his way around the tables, and Matt rolled his eyes, as he scooted over closer to the window so David could slide in. They all hurriedly pulled their coffee cups away from David as he put his portfolio down on the table, while Matt muttered, "You and your doodling."

Rose walked up to the table with her coffeepot, "Hiya, David. What'll it be this evening?"

"Evening, Rose – you look prettier each time I see you."

She winked, "*And,* I just started my shift – wait 'til you see me after I've put in a few hours on my feet."

Troy laughed, "If this rain keeps up, we just might be here to see that."

"Oh, we're here for a while," David smiled, "I've got some ideas for a journal of sorts that I wanna bounce off these guys."

They all laughed, knowing his penchant for turning random topics into marathon discussions and drawing sessions.

"You guys are gonna need a lot of coffee. Let me take your orders and I'll be back with the coffeepot. John, you've been the quiet one this evening, I'll start with you."

She took their dinner orders and headed for the kitchen. Before she was out of earshot, Troy called out to her, "Oh, Rose, Steve should be here shortly...he'll probably order everything on the menu." While they waited for their food, the four drank coffee and made small talk.

Rose returned carrying plates heaped with steaming man-food skillfully balanced on her arms. There was temporary chaos as David was forced to get his portfolio off the table to make room for meatloaf, country fried steak, mashed potatoes, and lots of hot bread. As Country Western music twanged in the background, the four friends enjoyed their hearty food and conversation.

As the plates were cleared, David pulled out his pencils and sketchbook. "So I'm starting my 'imaging' based on this story my dad used to read to me. Here's the 'what if'..." David opened a beat-up, leather pocket Bible and began reading the ancient story of Babel. He had already sketched out a rough tower before arriving.

> "Now the whole world had one language and a common speech. As people moved eastward they found a plain in Shinar and settled there. They said to each other, 'Come, let's make bricks and bake them thoroughly.' They used brick instead of stone, and tar for mortar. Then they said, 'Come, let us build ourselves a city, with a tower that reaches to the heavens, so that we may make a name for ourselves; otherwise we will be scattered over the face of the whole earth.' But the Lord came down to see the city and the tower the people were building. The Lord said, 'If as one people speaking the same language they have begun to do this, then nothing they plan to do will be impossible for them. Come, let us go down and confuse their language so they will not understand each other.' So the Lord scattered them from there over all the earth, and they stopped building the city. That is why it was called Babel – because there the Lord confused the language of the whole world." – Genesis 11:1-9

The post-story silence was gently broken as Matt laughed, "So you're telling me that a long time ago everybody on planet Earth actually spoke the same language? And somehow all

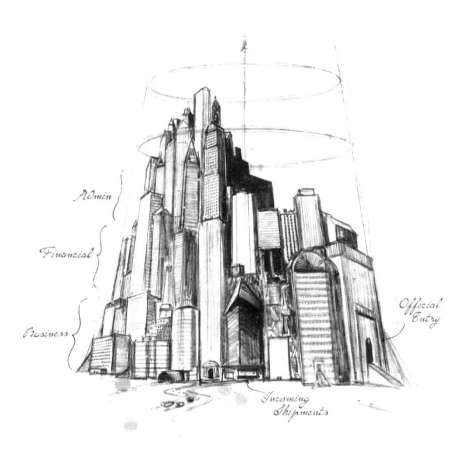

Admin
Financial
Business
Official Entry
Incoming Shipments

these ancient geniuses got together and decided to build the mother of all cities and then there was this...this tower that reached all the way to God....And then...like...boom...mass confusion of the tongues? And your point is...?"

David barely paused while shading in one of the tower's windows, "Well, obviously people never really stopped building cities and towers. They just did it on a smaller scale. All I'm saying is that, right now, we don't all speak the same language, but what would happen if that changed? What would happen if we *could* all speak the same language? What kind of 'towers' would we build? I just think it's an interesting supposition. Where would we go with it?"

John volleyed, "Well, we are still fixated on towers. I could see a huge tower becoming the hub of a political force. Look how much smaller the world has gotten these days. And the Web is the perfect propaganda broadcaster. Someday somebody's going to dream up a scheme for 'world domination' using the Internet...."

Matt looked skeptically at each of them, "Come on, John, you and your conspiracy theories. That's like a complete Dr. No fantasy. I work with technology systems every day, there's no way something like that could happen right now. You're talking about a world completely inundated by code. The majority of people around the world still don't even have a computer, much less an Internet connection."

"Glad I'm not 'Web-dependent,'" Troy said. "I don't need it to run my window-washing business; no big deal. That's what I like about window-washing. It's simple. It's low-tech."

"Troy, with all due respect, your cleaning business is dependent on computer systems; you just don't realize it. You put your money in a bank, and every bank uses the Internet these days. But as I keep saying, we've got a 'few more decades of coding' ahead before anyone can centralize control of..." Matt ticked off on his fingers, "banking, government, military, broadcasting, education."

"I just read that more people now have cell phones than toilets..." Troy joked.

Matt laughed, "What in the world are you reading these days!?"

David looked up, "Don't laugh, I read the same thing. You know better than I, Mr. Systems Engineer, that the power to process information is growing exponentially. Think of how much more digital information and data there is out there compared to ten years ago. You know it's being collected, analyzed, consolidated, and leveraged. You should know that, that's what you do! And...machines able to think like humans are not that far off, either. No one ever called me 'smart'; but now my close companion is a *smart* phone."

"Yeah, Skynet's going live next week," Matt retorted.

John added, "Aw...but there would have to be a series of catastrophes unlike anything the world has ever seen to really bring it all together...to really connect all the dots."

Worldwide economic crash

"Like what sorta things?" Troy asked.

"Well, first of all, it's got to impact *all* our money," John gestured with his hands. "You would need some sort of huge economic crash...we're talking worldwide. And, as we all know, we're pretty close to it with all the major economies being so interconnected. Right now, it wouldn't take much to set off the mother of all chain reactions... Boom! Boom! Boom, baby! You know, something that none of the nations could fix by themselves."

Matt continued his sarcastic interrogation, "The economy of entire nations collapsing in some sort of financial abyss sucking their middle class and the rule of law down with them, is that what you're saying?"

"Yes, and that followed by the nations who stupidly loaned them too much money," John added.

David furiously sketched a series of currency designs. "That cocktail would need a few more ingredients...like a global clash of ideologies without battle lines...every man, woman, and child on the face of the earth becomes a legit combatant."

Matt scoffed, "Why don't you throw in a natural disaster or two that would destroy not just a few thousand people but an entire population – your Old Testament sort of destruction. David! Why do you always have to be sketching when we talk?"

"Relax. Drawing's what I do..." He laughed, "The architect in me needs to see what I'm saying. And Matt – I respectfully disagree... I think it could happen...soon."

Troy added more possibilities, "How 'bout rogue nations – governments completely overrun by sheer evil – end-of-days outlaws who become human weapons of mass destruction?"

John jumped in, "Natural resources dry up...droughts, pestilence, famine; we're seeing that now."

Troy summarized, "So society collapses and a new system emerges that we discover we've been aiding and abetting all along: A *new* kind of system. A *new* way of controlling things and people."

"There you go." David flipped to another page and poised his pencil, "So what would be different for each of us if this all happened? How would we see ourselves?"

Matt leaned back and crossed his arms across his chest, "This is the stupidest thing I've ever heard...so keep talking."

David looked out the window, as a sudden gust of wind threw the rain at the panes, "I'm just asking...if we actually saw some sort of great catastrophe coming like a tsunami, how would it change us?"

Rose, who had been almost invisibly waiting to refill cups, chimed in, "That's kinda scary."

Matt growled, "No, that's kinda ridiculous."

"We're just talkin', man," John defended.

But the challenge was on and the verbal dueling was about to begin.

THE LAST TOWER

CHAPTER
02

THE UNRAVELING

"DO Y'ALL WANT ANYTHING ELSE, like dessert?" Rose's interruption shifted their attention to the menus she had thrust toward them as she started clearing the table. The diner was semi-famous for their pies. Each man chose his fruit or cream favorite before she left them again to their conversation.

Matt, as usual, fired the first volley. "How do you think this whole 'new tower syndrome' would start?"

There was a brief anticipatory silence. John responded with a pained expression on his face. "I think it actually started when the towers fell on 9/11; I'll never forget that, never. That was the day the world changed. A lot of people around the planet lost their innocence at that moment. I actually knew a few of the people who lost their lives that day – a corporate financier, a CPA, a friend from India – oh, and then there was this nice woman I once met in one of the offices – all gone now."

Rose bustled up to the table with a tray full of beautiful pie plates. "Need anything else right now?" They assured her that they were fine.

Taking the first great bite of strawberry pie loaded with whipped cream, Matt interjected, "Okay, so the world certainly has changed. Big deal, it's changed a lot over the past 300 years. You know, ever since the lights came on."

"You talkin' about the Enlightenment? The Age of Reason?" Troy asked.

"You guessed her, Chester." Matt grinned.

David frowned, "Matt, where has science and reason gotten us? We've just witnessed the bloodiest century in the history of civilization – along with a lot of science, technology, and utopian ideas. This was supposed to make us smarter and better. Anybody here think humanity has improved over the past several hundred years? New technologies have certainly put new powers into man's hands – but man's heart hasn't really changed. Sure, evil men existed in ancient times, but there was a limit to the threat they posed. Look at us now: One human finger on a button can terrorize or destroy tens of thousands."

John added, "Well, 9/11 certainly pushed us closer to the edge of an abyss, but the recent economic malfeasance – oh, let's call it what it is, just plain greed – has taken us to the edge of that abyss. The ugly reality is that many banks are now bled-out cadavers, and 'all the king's surgeons and all the king's men' can't stitch 'em up again."

Matt jumped in, "John, why do you have to be the world's most negative economist? Things are working out – they always do. The government rode in like the cavalry and rescued us."

"I know I'm being cynical," John admitted. "The government might have looked like the cavalry, but too little too late, man. We're surviving, but the game is over."

"What game?" Matt begged with a twinge of temper.

"It's not that long ago, when we could still play 'the real estate game'; then the bubble burst. We knew it wouldn't last, but who cared? It was great fun! Nobody was asking the tough questions. Later on, when the leaders said that they were all surprised by this crisis, it made no sense – at least not to me. We all knew back then that this real estate thing wouldn't last indefinitely. We just didn't know when the *whole thing* would go down."

Troy declared with a smirk, "So – the 'Great and Powerful Wizards' aren't all they're cracked up to be. Who's really in control here?"

David added thoughtfully, "I don't think anyone is in control right now... That's what's so scary."

John chimed in, "The idea that the banks could make money off of us – and then just pass *all* the risk on to an anonymous counterparty – is economics gone mad."

Matt put the question to John, "Is it true that they simply bundled all these toxic loans and just sold them off? How in the world could that happen?"

"Yes, it's called 'hide and seek.' You get a bunch of bad loans, mix them in with a few good ones and – whamo – you get triple A credit. Don't worry, guys, love is in the air. The big surprise is that you don't have to pay your mortgage back – well, not everybody anyway."

Matt sighed gloomily, "Well, at least some of the politicians seem to be using straight talk. I love it when they start resorting to terms like 'Economic Armageddon.'"

"That's not straight talk; they're just trying to put a scare into us so that we'll do whatever they tell us – that way the bailout will proceed with little or no resistance. 'Truth is the necessary medicine' and is going to taste pretty awful. Entitlements gotta be cut, revenues raised. Unless the straight talk includes 'sacrifice,' meaning a reduced standard of living, they're just trying to fool us!" John concluded.

Troy added, "Power, short-term profits, and political advantage sway the hearts and minds of many leaders. I've got a fable that illustrates the crux of the issue."

Matt grumbled because he knew Troy tended to be longwinded and once he started with a story he couldn't be stopped. Troy was a natural-born storyteller, and, after encouraging Matt to be patient, he began his tale. "Envision, if you will, this Virtual Tower as some grand estate, surrounded by the realm of imagination. Within this realm, wondrous farmlands and wealth-producing orchards flourish. One such orchard can even produce a crop of golden apples. This is an enterprise that is clearly profitable to its investors – in this case, the Goldholders. The scene opens early in the morning, as the sun shines down through the trees bearing golden fruit. Gathered in the midst of the orchard is a group of investors. Their attention is focused on a great scale erected to weigh these golden apples. The task before them is to determine the exact amount of gold that has been gathered over the past

Goldholders' meeting

year. When it becomes apparent to everyone that they have exceeded their goal, and are clearly satisfied with the results, the crowd begins to cheer. Yet this cheering abruptly stops when a young boy enters their midst – uninvited, of course."

"Hold on," John admonished, "I've attended shareholders' meetings. You had me until you brought the kid into the picture. That just doesn't happen – at least at none of the shareholders' meetings that I've been to."

Troy snapped back, "Yeah, well, that's the problem with too many shareholders' meetings. The families have no voice. They are stuck with whatever decisions the executives make."

As Matt sighed restlessly, Troy continued, "Please allow me to finish. The boy approaches the CEO and stands quietly before him. Some in the crowd notice that the boy has stuffed rocks in his pockets, and down the back of his shirt. Noticing the boy, the CEO addresses him in a condescending tone of voice, 'Well hello, young man, I'm the chief officer of this enterprise. And I'm curious, what are you doing here?'

"The child responds, 'Please, sir, won't you weigh me too?' Hearing this the crowd begins to laugh.

'Now, son,' says the CEO, 'why should I want to weigh you?!'

"'I heard my father say that you would be here today. He works in your orchard, you know. He says that you have come to weigh the gold and I figured, sir, if there was more weight you'd all be happier. I made myself heavier. I've got rocks in my pockets. I know it's not gold, but does that really matter? You know I want you all to be happy, because my daddy's afraid he's gonna lose his job if you're not happy.' Nobody laughs any longer."

The guys were now more attentive and seemed genuinely intrigued by what Troy was sharing; David was drawing intensely as he created more images from Troy's words. "The little boy clearly does not understand the purpose of this meeting. After an embarrassing silence, the CEO clears his throat, 'Perhaps you had better go home now to your daddy.' Dejectedly the boy hangs his head and walks back into the woods, scattering the rocks as he goes.

"Only a few weeks later, the Goldholders are informed in a conference call that the firm anticipates another year of ten percent growth. Now the management, knowing that this expectation may be difficult to realize, makes a decision to initiate across-the-board layoffs. The boy's father shows up for work one day, only to find out that he and several of his friends have been let go. Upon returning home and presenting the bad news to his wife and son, his little boy looks up at him and says, 'Daddy, I tried to help, but he didn't even ask your name.'"

After concluding his tale, Troy looked at each member of the group. "Is business only about making money? Is it right to shed people, not for survival, but for an extra penny of profit per share?"

John countered, "That thinking is not universal. For example shareholders in Japan are not given a status above employees, which is often the complaint we make against their markets."

"Well," Matt interjected, "funny you should tell this 'fable' as you called it. I just heard about a president of a large company

Going home to Daddy

and his Board of Directors who had been engaged in an approval process designed to provide a 40 million dollar bonus, payable directly to – guess who? – Mr. Big himself. At the same time, they chose this board meeting as an opportunity to lay off 10,000 people. Everything was perfectly justified by 'the data;' it was a company-wide business review."

"The news is not all bad out there. I know of a company that was facing significant layoffs due to market conditions. The leader talked to all the employees and proposed a different solution. He believed that when the market returned he would need the people back; so instead of significant layoffs, everyone would take a pay cut – starting at the top – to ride out the storm. Now that's leadership! My mind is boggled by the approval a market gives to leaders who initiate layoffs. Some of these become legends, but why do people get credit for layoffs? That seems like the easy path. The harder path requires creative thinking and imagination to find a way to reach financial goals and avoid layoffs. These are the leaders we should emulate."

Troy jumped in, "I'm not an executive and I don't know all the ins-and-outs of business, but I do see all around me families who suffer when a father or mother loses a job. Large companies should be required to present a Family Impact Report before any significant layoffs."

"Huh," grunted Matt.

"A report that would assess the impact on the community of these impending layoffs. Included in this report would be the cost to society and the number of children affected. Most developers are required by law to submit an environmental impact report. So I say: Give the children at least the same consideration as frogs and birds. Now, you can't make this the law for every mom-n-pop enterprise out there but it could be limited to those firms laying off, say, more than 200 people in a year, and it would be made public. As leaders consider the public relations implications of such a report, they might consider...uh...alternative solutions."

The bell above the door jangled as Steve walked in. He pulled up a chair beside the booth, and shook hands all around.

"Glad to have you back, Steve. Heard your Army Reserve unit was recently deployed to Japan for the tsunami disaster – what a tragedy," said David.

Steve nodded in agreement, "Oh, I've got plenty to talk about...but not right now – think I'll just eat and rest awhile. You can just talk at me. What have you guys been up to? You look kind of intense for this time of night."

"No, no. Nothing major. We're just talking about the world collapsing and Web sites the anti-Christ is visiting these days," feigned Matt with nonchalance.

Troy laughed. "Yeah, and David's got his pencil."

Rose arrived for Steve's dinner order, and the guys gave Steve a hard time as he did, indeed, order the meatloaf *and* the country fried steak. They had all heard that when he was growing up in Japan, wherever he went people patted his head and gave him candy, which made him sick, so he had to wear a sign on his back that read, "Please do not feed me." Nothing's changed; except now he needs a billboard.

As Steve glanced at David's sketches, Matt teasingly divulged some of the earlier conversational details, "Troy just finished telling us another one of his patented tearjerkers."

David showed Steve his sketch of the orchard with the golden apples, explaining Troy's point of view. Troy added, "We've been all over the map. We're speculating about what it would take to construct a global tower of power – bigger than the ancient Tower of Babel. Maybe there's an actual structure that exists somewhere that's tall enough to accommodate such power with all its global connections."

"Not gonna happen, dude. It'll be a network," Matt jabbed.

Steve looked a bit puzzled, "You guys talking about the tower in the Old Testament? You know I'm a structural engineer, right? It would take one mother of all foundations to support a tower like the one you are fantasizing about."

They all laughed. David conceded, "This tower is different. It would not be a single tower, but rather a collection of towers all interconnected virtually. Somewhere within the network, as Matt said, of this Virtual Tower there might conceivably be some kind of a central tower. Who knows?"

"Finally! You are agreeing with me," smiled Matt.

Steve mused, "Your idea of the tower reminds me of Megiddo of ancient times. This city was strategically located on the maritime route, the Via Maris, which passed through the Fertile Crescent, linking Egypt with Mesopotamia and Syria. Today, thanks to new technology, the trade routes around the globe can be managed from almost anywhere on the earth. The Internet would definitely be the key to your central 'Tower,' and it would become our new Megiddo."

"That is so geeky that you actually know all that without a Wikipedia cheat; I'm amazed you ever got a girlfriend," cracked Matt.

Rose was back with Steve's meal and cleared off the empty plates, leaving more room on the table for David to spread his drawings.

Troy, always nobly seeing things from the spiritual perspective commented, "'There is nothing new under the sun' – first you've got Megiddo, and now the Virtual Tower."

"You missed your calling, Troy," said Matt. "Shoulda been a preacher."

"Well, you know, there is a race today in the world to see who can build the highest structures." David was well versed in the cultural confidence – the wealthy façade – that height represents. It was a "manly man" way to distract, as it were, from the realities of poverty and hunger, which still burdened so many countries. "These structures are now soaring to dizzying heights, and, at the same time, taking on symbolic significance. Nations are using the latest technology to set new records. The Burj Khalifa in Dubai is the tallest, soaring a staggering 828 meters, and dwarfing its nearest rival, the Skytree in Tokyo. That one's an impressive 634 meters. There is the Shanghai World Financial Center, and Taipei 101 in Taiwan, and the world-famous Petronas Towers in Kuala Lumpur. Hundreds of towers and towering structures bristle from the face of the earth.

"Oh, and don't forget the Kingdom Tower, a planned development in Saudi Arabia. That's gonna be almost 1,000 meters. It'll be twice as tall as the Empire State Building, and for what? To attract more tourists who'll pay money simply to gawk at it. We should go climb a mountain instead." David was on a roll.

"Oh, and let's not forget the Burj Mubarak-al Kabir, that one's in Madinat al-Hareer, what they call the City of Silk. It's located in Kuwait. That tower's gonna beat them all. Its proposed height is over 1,000 meters."

The group paused in mild amazement at David's grasp of architectural masterpieces. Matt broke the silence, "Well, Mr. Walking Wikipedia, enough of this brick-and-mortar geeking.

Steve, tell us about this trip to Japan with your military reserve unit. Did you get to eat at an Iron Chef's restaurant?"

Troy chimed in, "Yeah, we used to hear a lot about the disaster in the news, but then, suddenly, the news just stopped. What's up with that?"

Steve leaned forward and rested his elbows on the table and got serious, "No lie, I will never forget seeing the devastation left by this tsunami. I tell you, the Japanese are a courageous people – the newspapers and TV gave you some idea of this. But the biggest story has yet to be told."

"What are you talking about, man?" quizzed John.

Steve addressed the group sternly, "I'll tell you what we've missed: Ever since man split the atom we have been on thin ice. And despite *all* our precautions we have lost control of the situation."

Mildly alarmed, Matt asked, "But they do have a handle on it, don't they?"

"Not really, they can barely see inside to get a clear picture of all four reactors. It's like a fire-breathing dragon – snorting flames and steam at the intruding cameras. I'm not kidding! The whole thing is crazy. Photo technology allows us to view beer cans in our backyards from space, yet our high-tech video camera can't see clearly inside the reactor's core."

At this point, Steve passed around a small picture booklet. "Here, I picked this up in Japan." Everyone looked at the booklet, which told the story. After a reflective pause, David speculated, "Anyone else seeing a pattern here? First, the Twin Towers fall, followed by the financial crisis, then comes

Mighty response from across Japan

多くの人が日本中から
被災地に駆けつけた姿に
感動しました。

Unknown heros sacrificed their lives for others

自分の命を犠牲にしてでも、
見えないところで
人を助けた人たちがいることを、
決して忘れたくありません。

Young & old put their lives at risk for the nation

命をかけて皆のために働く姿を知り、
頭が下がりました。

Children are the future

日本の未来は、
今ここに差し出された
愛の手の中にあります。

子どもたちを放射能から守ろうと
する多くのお母さんたちに対して、
私たちは、今も、これから後も、
どうすれば、その困難を分かち合う
ことができるでしょうか。
日本は間違いなく子どもたちの
安全を第一優先にし、新しい故郷を
子どもたちのために築き上げると
信じています。

A mother's trial

the mother of all waves, the great tsunami, and now we've got a fire-breathing dragon."

Matt clasped his hands in a prayer-like pose. "Please, please, please...no more conspiracy theories. And let's let Godzilla rest peacefully at the bottom of Tokyo Bay. I think we're all fine." As usual, he was not a big fan of alarmist notions.

Gesturing toward David, Troy exclaimed, "Our Wizards of Nuclear Science must be at their wits' end. It sounds like these reactors in Japan could present a danger to the entire country – not to mention the entire planet."

David responded, "Surely the Japanese people know what is going on." He turned to Steve, "Don't they?"

Steve declared, "Look, you guys, I've followed this story closely. At the moment the Japanese have only two weapons in their arsenal – limited disclosure and water. All the world's experts have concluded that the only immediate solution is to dowse the smoldering spent fuel with water, in an attempt to cool it down. Can you imagine, with all the available technology in the world – and with all the planning that must have gone into precisely this kind of contingency – that they are still left with only these two options – controlling the information flow and hosing the mess down with giant squirt guns?"

Steve expanded, "The question that still haunts me is whether those nuclear reactors can be safely maintained. It's not over yet; there are a few reactors that continue to pose a major threat. Better pray another earthquake with a magnitude of seven or eight doesn't hit. If it does, who knows what the hell will happen. The people fear the accuracy of the information coming from the government. Maybe the government fears full disclosure would set off a panic; but the people from the disaster area are strong and can handle full disclosure."

CHAPTER
03

THE FOREBODING

ROSE WAS BACK, REFILLING COFFEES and waters. After admiring the little Japanese booklet Steve showed her, she cleared away his empty plates as David posed another question, "What could possibly be dreamt up to go wrong next? We've already got the Big Financial Bust - the public has put the blame squarely on the shoulders of the Big Banks and the Fat Cat Industrialists."

John reacted, "Naw, people just took advantage of the available opportunities. Bad legislation is what set the table for the present state of affairs. Congressional Committees made a show of 'tar and feathering' certain targeted players, and then, after calling them on the carpet, winked and said, basically, 'Let's do lunch sometime.' This was all done for show, baby; the government hoped to deflect public anger, while at the same time restoring a modicum of trust in the financial sector."

David had little patience for such political games. "Imagine that – politicians spinning... This is unprecedented!"

Matt held his hands up in mock disgust, "It's easy not to trust them, but we've got to have a little more confidence in our government. It's gotten us out of trouble before, huh?"

"What planet have you been living on? You mean you actually still trust politicians? People are scared – they're losing money." David spoke with an uncharacteristic note of sarcastic annoyance, "There is no Great and Powerful Oz." He lowered his voice as deeply as he could make it, "Pay no attention to those men behind the curtain."

"The cynical view is that every banker is corrupt," Troy said, trying to ease some of the tension. "I don't agree with that view, but that's the general consensus. We're always too quick to judge others. Fact is, we have *all* contributed to this. Our inability to delay gratification lies at the core here."

John countered, "It may not be fair, but it sure is the perception. All these globalists, with their talk of restructuring the financial markets, have simply kicked the can further down the road in an attempt to buy a little more time."

Matt moved restlessly, "Buy time for what?"

"I don't know." John put his coffee cup on top of his dessert plate. "Maybe they need time to put in place the infrastructure and the rules for a...I hate to say it...New World Order."

Everyone groaned.

"No, seriously," John continued, "people don't respond when things are going okay; crisis is what galvanizes action. Sly pols don't tend to waste opportunities like that. But the odds of a serious, organized preemptive strike on the looming debt iceberg are low. So, in my view, a much larger crisis is just a matter of time."

Matt snorted.

David was adamant. "Leaders have promoted this over-reaching approach throughout history. The spirit of globalization is not modern. It's an old idea; it seems to be a regular passion of globalists."

John asked, "What happens the next time they mess up? The ol' Trust Tank is too low."

After a moment, Steve asked, "Could the next shock wave be triggered because no one, anywhere, is willing to pay the political price for a disciplined and comprehensive financial reform? I mean what happens when people realize their currency is no longer trustworthy?"

Matt shook his head sharply, "It won't be like that! The strong countries will help the weak ones."

"Look, Matt," John countered, "if you're talking about the Euro Zone, what you've probably been hearing might be a lot different from what's actually taking place. It may seem like the stronger members are trying to help the weaker ones, but in fact, they're just protecting their own backsides. The major players fear the contagion effect, which might pose a threat to their own economies if their weaker partner-countries default on loans. Integration and centralization provide some benefits, but when things start to turn sour, the after-effects can be devastating. The truth is, that as the EU begins to unravel, no institution is big enough to provide a liquidity backstop, and then the world falls off the cliff without a safety net or even a rope of hope."

Unemployment and the family

Steve was concerned, "Back to my question. What if people realize we're just playing with Funny Money?"

John raised his eyebrows, "Well, I guess we would have an old-fashioned global run on the banks, and guillotine treatment for all the rich bankers. Hell's bells, anyone that even looked wealthy might get strung up!"

Meanwhile, David sketched fervently, adding, "Since you all have brought up the matter – here's a scenario:

The unemployed

"A wealthy businessman, disturbed in the night by a knocking at his door, opens it to find a former employee standing silently before him. This man, clothed in a bathrobe, as if sleepwalking, gestures imploringly toward his home and now-destitute family in the nearby valley. What could this powerful man, taking in this scene, actually say? Sorry?"

John continued, "I can see it now: All the banks in the world closed overnight, and then the powerful globalists would appear on television with their spokesperson who would deliver a well prepared speech to calm the world." He sat up tall and fisted his hand in an authoritative gesture, "Everything is fine. All the banks will be reopening soon!" He slowly slumped back on the bench, "First, one week goes by...then two weeks...

"Money dries up, opportunities dry up... It's the flip side to Troy's Goldholders' meeting. Now jobs would *have* to be cut for company survival."

David started sketching out a dry riverbed, as Steve described his worries. "What would happen if a sharp disruption in the world banking system thrust even millions more into the unemployment lines around the world?"

He continued, "The only way to climb out of this dry place would be by the hand of a neighbor, friend, or family member. Social services would be non-existent. The streets would be filled with hungry people...desperate hungry people. The young who text their friends while sitting next to them will struggle in a chaotic world where convenience is replaced by survival instinct."

Troy added, "It's kind of scary when you think about what that thin blue line of the police prevents from happening. Democracy protects itself between anarchy and totalitarianism by thinking, voting citizens. No jobs, no pay, no government, no rule of law...no civilized society."

THE LAST TOWER

CHAPTER
04

FIAT CURRENCIES

One world currency

ROSE SWUNG PAST TO CHECK on the table again, and topped off their water glasses before moving off to another booth. "Look, this money we are presently using to operate our global economy is only as good as the trust people have in themselves and in the economic strength of their respective countries. This fiat currency is backed by the sobering words from the government, 'It shall be done.' These words alone suffice to persuade a gullible electorate that their money is indeed sound. The people are led to believe they are in good hands. This currency's value is based not on its convertibility to any tangible standard, but simply on the declaration made by the government. It is assumed that the public will not question this assertion."

John moved his cup and plate again, "Money is backed by a nation's wealth and credibility. When you," he waved his hand in a circle, "and other people around the globe lose trust in your own economy, and similarly begin to distrust the State, you will dump your paper money in exchange for something tangible. The risk is a cascading contagion; this is what world powers fear the most. Control is critical to wealth and power. Look at what just happened in Egypt when they lost control of the masses."

Troy responded, "So everyone shuts their eyes, pretending they can grow out of the problems. Everybody knows that there is one thing that remains for the West yet to learn: Remember the tale by Hans Christian Andersen?"

John remarked, "Don't tell me – *The Emperor's New Clothes*?"

Troy said, "You've got it! Nobody but some little kid had the honesty to tell the Emperor that he was actually naked. Somebody must convince the West that we too are naked – the party's over."

David tweaked a couple of lines on his tower sketch. "In order to attain their awesome height, these ziggurats had to be built in the form of a great spiral structure, twisting heaven-ward; people created towers and temples that purported to be a spiral road to God. Round and round and round you would go as you approached the summit of one of these artificial mountains. The Chaldeans and Sumerians who con-structed these things expressed their worldview in the design. If we could get a look inside, we would see that our tower is honeycombed with all sorts of passages and staircases leading nowhere...shafts, pitfalls, and various other bureaucratic, architectural features."

"Congrats, you are maintaining your commanding lead in the Walking Wikipedia Race," Matt snapped.

John spun the tale a little more while holding a sketch of currencies David had made. "One of the more interesting features of this Tower would be its ability to issue a new world currency – one allegedly backed by gold or some other valued resource. The credibility of the Tower would now be unassailable. The press would claim that the Tower's 'goldmine' holds unlimited potential. The public would regard this as their entitlement, their inheritance if you will, from planet Earth."

Matt groaned, "Oh please…"

John continued, "And, if we expand this scenario, in the midst of an economic crisis, the Tower now has an answer: Provide a means for a currency exchange – a one-time opportunity to swap your old worthless currency and the gold and silver you possess for this new Star Currency."

"Oh, I like this," David murmured, and started detailing rivers of gold flowing from the Tower.

Steve grinned, "You're enjoying this a little too much, David."

John, with his logical accountant's mind, suddenly saw all the connections. His thinking was altered along the lines of Jules Verne. "Everybody jumps at the chance to make the swap. Remember, the banks are closed; there's a food shortage. What they don't know is that this 'goldmine' is just a propaganda ploy. All those hopefuls with delusions of grandeur have just sold the 'family cow' for a 'handful of beans' – and they ain't magic beans."

Steve questioned him on this point, "Matt's right, who would believe such nonsense? Who would swap their money for something as crazy as that? You, the bean-counter…*Jack and the Beanstalk*? Where are you getting this stuff?"

John nodded. "Context, lad! This time, the press expands their coverage into a major campaign with headlines

Flowing rivers of gold

proclaiming: *Largest Goldmine Discovered.*" He swept his hand out in emphasis. "The whole scheme is now 'foolproof.' The New World Order assures the public that it has the economic situation in hand."

Troy muttered, "'Fool's Gold.'"

John reminded them, "Context, context, context... All the banks are closed. You can't buy food; you can't pay for anything. You're stuck and someone comes to you with this grand crazy idea. I'll bet a lot of hungry people would jump at it."

Matt was exasperated, "Man, you're really talking crazy crap."

John defended his position. "What I'm talking about isn't pretty, but hear me out! Debt is bearing down on you: your mortgage, the kid's education. You can't see your way to paying it back. Now...poof...you trade your debt for your share of the goldmine, all your debt and all your problems disappear like magic. Reset...it's ingenious. Bow to your Sensei!"

Steve responded, "Well, given those circumstances, I might actually see this taking place. I would probably do the deal if everyone else were doing it. The party could continue; all would be forgiven. I know of fiscal conservatives who, when they hit hard times, quickly shift their loyalties."

Troy reiterated, "I still wouldn't be fooled by that scenario. I can envision an alternative global solution. It would require the globalization of all the major natural resource reserves of the entire world: gold, oil, timber, silver, even fresh water. All currencies of the world would be converted into a new 'unsinkable' World Currency solidly backed by these natural resources. The banks would reopen, and – except for those companies whose resource reserves had been confiscated – the markets would surge. Hope would be restored but the Tower would reserve the right to make any new rules."

John added, "The real time bomb lurking behind the 'lull before the storm' would be the smoldering anger over the wealth gap. Those in the upper echelon would assume that others would want to get their hands on this upper-crust wealth. Those working on the lower levels would feel neglected, because they would not be getting a fair share of the Tower wealth. Then you'd have those leaders who continually exacerbate the wealth gap in the attempt to further divide us for their own political gain. To exert its control, the Tower managers would have to deal with this problem. I mean this is why certain Middle Eastern countries start handing out checks to the citizenry the moment there's rebellion in neighboring states."

Steve retorted, "Let's take a look at home. Politicians in the US are also into this business of buying loyalty. They print more money and buy votes with short-term policies. This is really just a reverse image of Robin Hood – taking from the future generation in order to shore up the present standard of living of *this* generation. Naturally, such a policy would enhance a politician's chances for reelection. So what is the difference between stealing from the future generation and stealing from a local bank?"

David reflected, "Okay, I get it! The Tower o' Power won't let the gap expand. They will print more money, and give credit, even to those who do not have the ability to pay the loans back – anything to keep a lid on the simmering tension between the haves and the have-nots."

Troy reasoned, "I sense a certain irony here: When we die, we leave our wealth behind us. I'll bet no one would cry out from his deathbed, 'I wish I had accumulated more stuff.' His final regret would probably be, 'I wish I had spent more time with my family.' God is the great Equalizer. We are all created equal – that is to say, we are created in His image. When it comes to things like fairness, it is out of our hands. This is one of those things in life that we cannot understand, just like how He allows suffering. All I can say is that I believe that God loves us."

Matt slapped the table, "Troy, if there were a preacher's version of *American Idol,* you would probably win. Just try to tell the guy who lives from paycheck to paycheck that he's on par with those living in the mansions in the Hamptons, or in the waterfront properties in Naples, Florida. They'll all just laugh at you."

Steve jumped in, "Well, it's actually not so much about how much you have, as it is about what you do with it, right? Hoarding treasure is just plain counterproductive. Isn't there a parable in the Bible about the danger of obsession with building bigger barns? David, sketch me a barn, will you?"

David began to sketch a rich man's horde, while attempting to diffuse the tension between Troy and Matt. "Okay, okay; so the Tower will continue to print more and more money in order to keep everybody happy. But it won't work for long. In the meantime, they'll have to come up with yet another scheme."

Hoarding treasures

Now Matt leaned back, trying to get a handle on the discussion, "So, this New World Order will be one of fantasy and illusion, with immediate gratification coming from fool's gold? I wish I could believe in fantasy and science fiction, but hey, I've got to get back to planet Earth now."

John tossed the sketch of the currency back on to the table. "I can actually picture the ultimate financial crisis, with its sky-high, unpayable debt, food riots, thugs – black market economy – the works. We're just now seeing the tip of that iceberg."

Steve agreed, "The dark tower initiates the biggest money grab in the history of the world. Hey, we should probably talk about this stuff at the bar. I could use a drink about now."

THE LAST TOWER

CHAPTER
05

THE RESOURCE GRAB

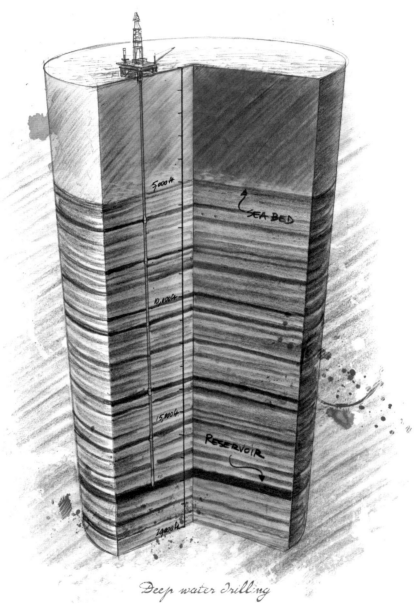

5,000 ft

SEA BED

10,000 ft

15,000 ft

RESERVOIR

20,000 ft

Deep water drilling

O WHEN DO YOU THINK the 'black gold' resources from under the sea and earth are going to be tapped out?" David asked mischievously.

Steve answered, "Soon, because whatever plays out in the next wave of destruction has to be, in some way, energy-related. We've been going through oil like it'll last forever, but the energy prophets of doom love screaming that it is running out…and they're probably right! Some believe that, in terms of oil production, the Saudis' best days are behind them. You start to wonder about the validity of our so-called 'proven reserves' in the world's oil supply. You just know the disaster in Japan, with the shutdown of all the nuclear reactors across the country, is just a little peek into the growing demand for diminishing supplies of fossil fuels."

David stopped drawing, "You can see the battle lines being drawn as the grab for resources heats up. From the South China Sea through the East China Sea, boundary disputes are erupting; everybody's flexing their muscle, and those without muscle are crying foul. The raw emotions of nationalism, religion, and money are a toxic combination that can lead to serious trouble."

Matt worried, "Yup, Colonialism: Part II. There's a reason why all these potentially dangerous military maneuvers are carried out across the entire globe. The easy oil days are over; we gotta go deeper to find it, probe boundaries, test treaties. Once oil is tied to a nation's survival, the ante goes up. Nations will fight for resources and to keep the sea lanes of commerce open."

Tapping his finger on the table, David added, "And the US is in no position to say much about this, since we've been the greatest oil grabber in history."

Steve responded, "Look, all the big industrialized countries roam the world, cutting deals with any little nation possessing potential reserves, even if those nations have a poor record on human rights. They do whatever is strategically important for their own interests and survival. We're very Darwinian when it comes to oil exploration."

John turned to Steve, "Are you siding with critics who claim that the recent wars we've been fighting were more about oil than about terrorism?"

Steve set him straight, "No, I'm not saying that at all. Look, there are more ways to get your neighbors' resources than by waging war. Money is actually the preferred weapon of choice."

He continued, "Energy independence still has to be the Holy Grail. We are going to have to get serious about conservation, but that alone won't get the job done. Even as we get some traction toward renewable energy, we've still got to drill at

home. Dependence on foreign oil supplies puts our economy in the hands of some pretty unscrupulous guys."

"That's great, now you sound like an Exxon commercial," quipped Matt.

David held one of the mini-picture books from Japan. "Well, I don't think we're going to be building any nuclear plants anytime soon."

John surmised, "Countries are still looking seriously at alternative paths to energy and energy independence, but I say it's way too late. It takes time to develop safe alternative resources."

Troy once again spoke through the prism of his worldview, "Are you referring to solar power and wind energy? These are examples of renewable resources, and my own uncle, who happens to be a farmer, always thanks God for these natural resources: sun, wind, and rain. Without proper respect for nature and our Creator, we're going down the wrong road with this energy problem.

"My uncle and his dad have been tied to the land and his wife and mother have been tied to the home. Their story is a simple, yet impressive one."

Matt interrupted, "How long a story is it and are you going to talk about anyone named Wilbur or Jed?"

"Matt, I want to hear this! Let him finish," barked David, still sketching.

Troy continued, "My Uncle Brian has a 200-acre farm in Wisconsin, along with the family home that's been there since his great-grandparents built it."

Rose and her coffeepot interrupted the story. As she cleared off the rest of the table, they decided to order some salty, savory items off the appetizer menu...a reverse palate cleanser after the pie. Matt rolled his hand to continue, "Okay, Troy, let's finish your story."

"My uncle always told me that growing crops was like a miracle. There's no guarantee, but if the rains come at the right time, and if the sun shines, and if you put your heart into your work, these seeds planted in the dark soil will someday burst forth into the light – it's all part of God's plan."

"I would respectfully like to point out that it's just Mother Nature doing her thing, not some cosmic force magically sprouting a kernel of corn," Matt interrupted.

Troy quietly pushed back. "Well, my point is that he said that he learned from his father to always give thought to tomorrow. My Grandpa Bill even planted an oak tree near the farmhouse as a sign that you should always leave something good for the

Wisconsin farm

Knitting children's blankets

future generations, and his favorite saying was: 'The most important legacy is the effect you have on the lives of people.'

"My Grandma Judy is just like that, too. Her pastime was spent knitting children's blankets. The first of these blankets were intended for her grandchildren, but as she got up there in years, she continued to knit those blankets. Now these were for the unborn – those great-grandchildren and great-great-grandchildren whom she actually would never meet. Her sacrifice and love were such that it eventually led to a crippling effect on her hands, requiring surgery.

"All I'm saying is, our use of natural resources should take into consideration our grandchildren and all the great-great-grandchildren we've got coming."

Matt grinned, "You know, Troy, sometimes your stories actually make sense to me. I like that one."

Wheel of the Middle Class
The mid-level wheel

A S ROSE SWUNG PAST THE group's table yet again, David found himself watching her as she moved around the booths and tables. "She really circles the room regularly, doesn't she?"

Earlier he had found himself drawing a new series of pictures around this notion almost before the concepts were fully developed in his head. "Take a look, guys. These wheels, each rotating on its own axis yet all linked together, are a reflection of life on Earth...an endless cycle that, in the great scheme of things, never fixes all the social ills that are inextricably part of its makeup. Gotta work, and work hard, to keep the wheels turning: The wheels of industry, the wheels of government, the wheels of finance, along with the 'grease' of law and the wheels of justice."

Rose's distinctive chuckle rippled over their conversation and they looked over as her table of customers laughed at her reply. David smiled, "Some people work with a purpose and see meaning in their work, regardless of what it is. Others see no purpose in their work at all, and round and round we go, rodent-like, running in some giant hamster wheel with no means of escape; it is the nature of life in our very flawed world."

He pointed to one of his pictures. "Look at this large wheel. Call it the Wheel of the Middle Class. Check out the motivations they have for working."

Steve was impressed by the speed with which David could illustrate his ideas, "Let me see that... Nice work!" The others nodded.

He pointed out, "And remember, our Tower is global; people in developing countries are moving into the middle class in larger numbers. These folks spend money on education, their ticket to the middle class. Once there, they embrace their middle class status by buying lots of stuff. This is the primary engine of growth in the world today."

Matt agreed, again, "The trick is to keep large segments of the citizenry trained in an essential growth field for the future. Some companies train their people for new growth fields, while others lay them off without providing such training. Jobs are flowing out of the United States like water, seeking the lowest level of cost-effectiveness. Many of these jobs are not coming back, so you gotta wonder if the American dream is over for a lot of people."

Finishing another wheel, David declared, "This one's even larger. Let's call this the Wheel of the Working Class. Picture an underground wheel, encompassing the entire earth. Some of these people are literally underground workers. They bring to the surface those raw materials needed to run the Tower – these materials could be precious gems and resources like

Working class wheel
The service wheel

oil, iron ore, and coal. Then, you'd have the waitresses, cooks, launderers, and janitors. Of course, it's not all cut and dried. There is a seamless connectivity between the wheels; not a big chasm between them. As an example, you could have a blue-collar small business owner running a million-dollar cleaning business. Is he in the middle class or lower class?

A waitress on the service wheel

These distinctions aren't set in stone; nor are they necessarily important. Ultimately, it comes down to what the individual thinks."

Troy tapped one of the people that David had drawn. "Listen, man's dignity isn't found in his job description, or with the label that society gives him, but in his sense of self-worth. A janitor who works hard at the most menial tasks, and encourages those around him to do likewise, makes a much greater contribution to society than a rich man running a selfish course."

Steve honed in on the wording, "You're right. 'Class' is the wrong word to use in the titles of these wheels. It's not class, but service and impact. The largest wheel houses the masses of humanity that are routinely overlooked. Their work is an absolutely essential part of the world's economy. In fact, their efforts sustain the world, but too often we take them for granted."

"I agree!" And David crossed off the titles he had written on his sketches and retitled them.

His pencil was now practically flying across the page, revealing a very ornate wheel. "Look at this one; this one is moved by the powerful and the influential."

He looked up at John, "Your education and business connections have placed you among those in the upper level management. You work on the same wheel with the intellectuals who work to determine the future world order, my friend. This wheel extends into the sky itself, moving more rapidly than the other wheels; its momentum and power are gained from the lower wheels, which multiply and increase its speed."

Troy added, "The bottom line is that we still retain a division of labor. That doesn't mean that we, the people, are divided. Okay, so we're on our respective wheels, but these wheels are all connected; that just means we need each other, right? Each worker, in his own way, contributes value, though we are certainly not rewarded with equal pay."

David continued, "Those who wish to divide us by putting everything on the basis of wealth are simply misguided; we need a balanced point of view. I personally believe the wealth gap has to be reined in, but class warfare is not the answer. We can't continue to endure that sucking sound, the sound of capital being consumed by the Ivory Tower. A small, elite group cannot be allowed to monopolize capital, like a kid who dominates the game of *Monopoly*. This is a formula for disaster that will eventually unleash the wrath of the masses. It's happened before, you know...."

John looked at David and asked a question central to the discussion. "Okay, I get the idea of this interconnected series of wheels, but my question is this: Are you implying that all our work is futile, that we go round and round and are essentially going nowhere? And this is going to be part of the downfall of our current 'Tower'?"

Matt bristled, "What are you saying about 'intended purpose and common laborers' here? You're talking about some God-thing, aren't you?"

David gently responded, "Matt, there really is no such thing as a common laborer; we are all unique, and real purpose in our work adds meaning to our lives."

Acknowledging David's point, Matt flipped through some of the pictures he had drawn. "I've got a question. Just who might these people be, these managers of this Virtual Tower, who will somehow invent ingenious ways to keep us on our respective wheels?"

John answered, "Well, I'd imagine that any leader who aspired to rule the world would most likely come from the elite of the Upper Wheel, an Ivory Wheel, if you will. Many

Ivory wheel

of these movers and shakers would surely share a common passion for centralizing authority. For others, as we've said, money would be the motivation. And still others might hold a sincere belief that centralized authority is needed to save the planet. Nevertheless, all great empires relied on some form of authority."

Building on this, Steve asked, "But where are these great empires today? The Persians, the Romans, and the Mongols? The British and French Empires were huge. Nazi Germany and the Soviet Union continued the quest for world domination in the 20TH century. Today, we have the United Nations, the International Monetary Fund, and the World Court all attempting to be the arbiters of world order. So, in place of the *Pax Romana*, we now have the *Pax Americana*."

Troy added, "History is littered with examples of leaders gone mad – so crazy that they actually thought they were gods and that they could control the world."

Matt asserted, "Yup, Mussolini said, 'It's blood that moves the wheels of history.' And lots of people seem to want to make history these days."

John wondered, "Hey, Troy, it still bothers me, if God is in control then why is the world falling apart? Why would we be left with this Tower and entertaining the prospect of a New World Order to solve all our problems?"

Troy tilted his head down a bit, "John, I honestly don't have an answer for why God allows suffering and pain. I know it's a cliché you hate but an omnipotent, omniscient God is not confined to our understanding or logic. And yes, I know that sounds a bit cruel, but think about it. A lot of times there are just no answers; there's just God. I simply believe He loves us. His ways, awful as they may seem so often, are under His divine control and plan. Someday we will understand far more than we do today."

"And *that's* your conclusive argument?" replied Matt in mock awe.

Suddenly, Rose's voice broke into the conversation:

I met a traveller from an antique land
Who said: "Two vast and trunkless legs of stone
Stand in the desert. Near them, on the sand,
Half sunk, a shattered visage lies, whose frown
And wrinkled lip and sneer of cold command
Tell that its sculptor well those passions read
Which yet survive, stamped on these lifeless things,
The hand that mocked them, and the heart that fed.
And on the pedestal these words appear:
'My name is Ozymandias, King of Kings;
Look on my works, ye mighty, and despair!'
Nothing beside remains. Round the decay
Of that colossal wreck, boundless and bare,
The lone and level sands stretch far away."

The men stared up at Rose in shock! She grinned confidently as she set out the next round of food that they all ordered. "I had to study Percy Shelley in high school – I found *Ozymandias* fascinating."

"That's impressive," David said with a smile.

John pushed the conversation back on point, "Now look, not every person on the Ivory Wheel is a ruthless Hitler

The award for excellence...

wannabe. We all have our own personal demons to contend with, and we're all misunderstood, right? We can all fall prey to the power thing. Let me tell you a true story. I was recently invited to a banquet where a close friend of mine was being honored.

"This ceremony was attended by many of my peers – you know, the guys in the Upper Wheel. My friend was being presented with one of those dumb 'career-building special awards.'

"He's a really good guy! He would do anything for any of you here. He's just messed up, but he's no different from the rest of us. He later told me that he both loved and hated this award. He said that flattery can never be trusted, and that everyone is probably looking for some kind of connection with him. Ended up hating the praise, but couldn't live without it. At times, he's

Praise is like the wind; it's fleeting and fickle.

The monkey dance

felt himself going mad from the pressure – you know, the stress of meeting performance standards. He came home from that awards banquet really troubled. The whole celebration seemed like one big farce."

Matt jumped in. "Let me tell you another story. I don't intend to mention any names here, but there once was this young man, full of potential, a good kid. He loved his parents, but, once he set in motion his ambitious life plans, he no longer had time for his father and mother. I knew that one of his professors, perhaps the best teacher he'd ever known, had really helped him along, and that guy learned a lot and developed intellectually. Now, the prof tells me that he hasn't contacted him once since graduation. The boy, well, now a man, had the nicest wife, one who worked hard when they had nothing. But no sooner did his career take off, sure enough, he found himself another woman." Matt turned angry, "And that was probably the biggest mistake of his life. He'll never find a woman as wonderful as my daughter.

"I'm sorry; I said I wasn't going to mention any names. So, now you know. Anyway, he finally achieved his goal: Unlimited access to those in power. He'd do whatever they asked him to do; it's like they were gods to him. I can't reveal exactly what happened but let's just say it's as absurd as telling a grown man to 'dance like a monkey.' So dance he did. He simply let his lust for advancement get the better of him. Now he sits in a jail cell. The second wife recently deserted him." Again, Matt fought to hold onto his emotions.

"But my daughter still continues to visit him faithfully. It just breaks our hearts."

THE LAST TOWER

CHAPTER
07

BABEL II

Virtual tower

WHILE THE FOUR FRIENDS MURMURED their consolation to Matt, his cell phone suddenly rang, startling everyone. Matt chuckled, "It's amazing how these electronic gizmos run our lives." Matt picked up, while John excused himself. The rain steadily continued to come down and the streetlights beyond the window were reflected on the wet pavement. Troy took the opportunity to close his eyes for a few minutes, and David added some additional details to the pictures he had so hurriedly been drawing, while Steve perused some older sketches from David's portfolio.

Matt, finishing his phone call, looked sheepishly at the other men, "Sorry about that...my wife..." Looking down at the device in his hand, he shook his head, "Now, there's a change for you. Yep, we've come a long way since clay tablets and pay phones – and everything's interconnected."

"As you recall," David began doodling satellites around his Tower, "it was human pride and a common language that got the people of Babel into trouble with God. We have a similar situation emerging here – the computer has become the universal interpreter, and it will allow anyone with Internet access to speak to anyone else anywhere in the world."

John clapped his hands as he slid back into the booth, "This sure sounds like Babel: Part II is coming!"

Pointing to David's satellites, Troy said, "And like Nimrod shooting his arrows into the sky, we send up rockets with satellites. Tower-Stars, that's what we should call them."

"Who's Nimrod?" asked Matt.

"Some traditions say that he was the king who actually built the Tower of Babel," Troy answered. "Tradition also says that he built the tower and shot arrows into the sky to challenge God. Kind of like shaking his fist and daring God to send another flood."

David sketched out a muscular ancient warrior with six-pack abs launching a satellite from a bow, "The things we shoot into the skies today have become indispensable for enabling a global language of sorts. And naturally more governmental control."

"How advanced is our present technology for enabling this common global language?" John wondered.

Matt leaned forward, "The key to this Tower idea of yours would have to be the computer – massive mainframes that would gather, record, and analyze all the information flow of the world. To be honest, the only legit answer to the world's economic problems will probably require incredibly complex computerized coordination and central planning. There would have to be a huge global solution with enormous amounts of accurate information."

Nimrod launching satellites

David filled in details to his throwback sci-fi sketch of a large mainframe computer room as John suggested, "The management of the Virtual Tower would become the computer's gatekeeper. Purportedly to ensure accuracy and safety in information flow, they would eventually have to provide monitoring and oversight constraints for what was allowed over the network."

Troy worried, "Computers are machines. They have the conscience of a chainsaw. They cut and control what they are

Computer servers

told to cut and control. For instance, drones have a potential for good and a grand potential for some pretty diabolical schemes, when you think about it."

"You do realize," Steve speculated, "that those in the Tower would need to control everything in order to maintain order and power. Machines could monitor words and phrases, and I think that anyone inputting anything from a pipe bomb recipe to a religious expression of faith would find his words being scrutinized by the code. There could be enormous control through technologies originally designed to benefit and protect us."

John agreed, "People input, calculate, evaluate, and react to the data. People make decisions. We are probably going to be held accountable by machines for everything we say that we take for..."

Matt reacted, "Guys, guys...you're going nuts with this conspiracy stuff. This is worse than being at a family reunion with my mother's crazy sisters."

John warned, "No, Matt, herein lies the risk of being overly enamored of any technology, when we do not objectively look at its potential for evil as well as good."

Matt remained unconvinced, "Well, from where I'm standing, I'd say a lot of people are pretty pleased with the convenience and ease offered by this technology. It has advanced the economy, education, medicine, etc., etc., etc. It's simply an interactive tool for communication, a means for people to join together, enabling them to promote and build a lot of great projects on a global scale. What are you guys, a bunch of fuddy-duddy Luddites?"

Steve replied, "Anything employed to meet human needs and interests is great. But what if technology is used to target specific sectors of the population that think or behave in a manner considered contrary to a New World Order agenda?"

David turned to a fresh page in his sketchbook and began sketching while he talked, "I've been thinking that the whole operation would be so complex and far-reaching that it would require more than just uniformity of language."

Matt asked suspiciously, "I'm almost afraid to ask what you mean by that..."

Hall of conformity

"I think they would want unity of thought – you know, *Groupthink*. They wouldn't want other ideologies competing with their own.

"Look, here's a sketch of a hall. Let's call it the Hall of Conformity – it stands adjacent to the great Ivory Wheel. Let's use this hall as a symbol for ensuring compliance, efficiency, and safety, so as to meet all the Tower's requirements. The computer could now become the arbiter of accurate info and, eventually, truth; and since the managers control the programming of the computer, truth would be whatever they wanted it to be."

"When did you become the reincarnation of George Orwell?" laughed Matt.

John grinned at Matt, "Soooo...you don't think the computer's capability for evil is as great as David suggests?"

Matt responded, "Not like that! Maybe when it comes to porn...but rule the world!?! Give me a break. The computer is an amazing tool. It has been used for great good, which far outweighs any imagined applications for evil. As I said before, look at *all* the benefits having this much information at hand has brought to the world.

"Okay, so maybe a potential threat could hang over our heads; I can see that there could be a dark side to the masters of this technology as well. However, I don't believe that technology itself presents a major risk. I actually see this issue of enforced conformity as being far more complex than you are fantasizing about right now."

"Well, who says conformity is necessarily evil if it's for the greater good?" Steve wondered. "It does aid efficiency. We need *some* rules."

Troy conceded Steve's point, "I agree, some degree of social conformity is necessary for the greater good. But when does conformity cross the line into coercion?"

David explained in an almost clinical tone, "The managers of the Tower could resort to many control options. History has not been silent on this point. Caesar taught us the strategy of controlling people with bread and circuses. Stalin demonstrated the primeval approach with mass murder and gulags located in faraway places – also quite effective."

Steve interjected, "Well, in Japan, there is a story which illustrates various strategies for control. This story is about three great warlords. It concerns a bird in a cage. One warlord says, 'If the bird doesn't sing, kill it.' Another says, 'If the bird doesn't sing, make it sing.' And the third one says, 'If the bird doesn't sing, wait for it to sing.'"

Matt regarded Steve with some puzzlement. "Sorry, Stevie, I don't exactly follow you on that one, but I get the general picture."

David reentered the conversation, "Okay, guys, with technology the new authorities could say, 'We know where you are and what you are doing at any moment, so we advise you to comply with our rules.' The possibilities for control are limitless. Of course, those authorities couldn't reach our heart and soul... or could they?"

John broke the intermittent silence, "Well, if anyone controls our thoughts, it won't be because of technology, but because we've let our minds go soft. Hours are spent each day listening to people who tell us how things should be. We are entertained morning and night, without critically thinking as to where all this is leading, and we don't ask the hard questions. We are enamored of anyone with a 'feel good' story. It doesn't matter whether their words have ever been tested. We give our vote for a cheap promise and place our kids' future in untested ideas. I sometimes wonder how much independent thinking remains. Have our minds already been seduced by the 'tube'? Guys, there are forces that are playing with our brains."

Troy was visibly frustrated, "All this talk of sovereignty and authority; the computer is not God!"

Matt answered sarcastically, "Exactly! But computers, at present, pretty much know everything that legally pertains to us. They know our buying habits, and you don't tell 'em 'no.' They know more about us than we do about ourselves. Someday, we'll have a microchip implanted somewhere, so the computer can scan us. No more credit cards. No more overdrafts. It won't allow it."

Troy mused with a sly smile, as if he knew something, "So we can all buy and sell, so long as we carry this chip or...'mark,' huh?"

"Yeah... Anything wrong with that?"

"Plenty. The Star Currency alone would be insufficient to control and guarantee the economic order. I imagine there would have to be some enforcement mechanism. To access the 'goldmine,' people would need some kind of a code to prove they are entitled to it – and playing by all the rules, of course. So only those who are compliant could actually buy food."

David expanded on this general concept, "The food weapon would force many to conform to the rules. If you can't induce them to follow, you coerce them to do so."

Matt shot a valid point, "But wouldn't people eventually catch on and rebel against the system?"

Steve said flatly, "Not if they're hungry, they won't."

John observed, "Most people love convenience – one-stop shopping. People are more than happy to receive a new identity number if it gives them more convenience and buying power. Shape and form are almost irrelevant as long as it's not... inconvenient. You just need a big personality and a good story to persuade them."

Steve suddenly leaned back from the table and stared up at the ceiling as if caught up in some kind of reverie. "Ya' know, all this talk about atomic power, and energy resources... Where would this Tower be without the energy grid – you know – electric power? The 'choke' point of the Tower's power *is* the grid."

This suddenly aroused Matt's undivided attention. "Just what are you getting at, Steve?"

"Well, it's just like this, Matt, you probably know more about this phenomenon than I do... It's called a solar flare – what some folks call 'sun spots.' They can wreak havoc with electrical devices and navigational equipment. Right?"

Matt eyed Steve cautiously, "Yeah, but Steve, are you implying that this Tower of yours – if it's ever built – can be brought down by an act of nature?"

"Maybe an act of God," Steve persisted.

"If the people won't rebel against the Tower, if the Tower takes our children from us and throws them into 'Tower-run schools' and intimidates us, maybe – just maybe – the Tower's power could be knocked off its throne by the *sun*. Picture this – a huge display of the 'Northern Lights' just before dawn, and then the entire electrical grid goes down – a result of a series of massive geomagnetic solar storms. Waves of solar flares arrive unabated. GPS satellites knocked out, travelers stranded and dispersed across the globe, telecommunications disrupted. There goes the Tower and its 'utopia.' We'd all be in the dark – scattered once again."

Troy shrugged, "So, the Tower goes down. Big deal – let it. The silver lining in the whole dark thing would be this: The children would finally come home to their families.

"We'd have nothing; but we would have *everything* – and we could once again build something that really mattered."

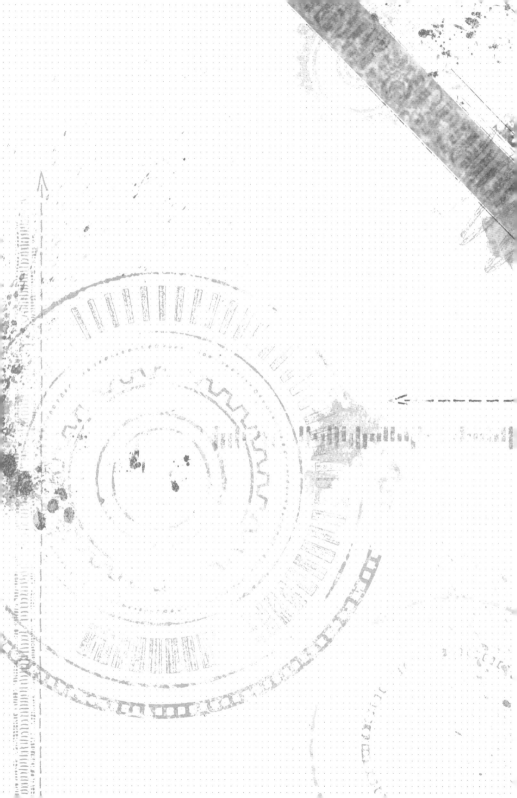

THE LAST TOWER

CHAPTER
08

THE CRYSTAL TREE

Crystal tree

ROSE INTERRUPTED AT THIS POINT to tell them that her relief had arrived, nodding her head vaguely in the direction of a young woman refilling the coffee urns. "More coffee before I hit the road?" As the men moved their cups over toward her, some of David's drawings fell off of the table. She bent down to pick them up. "Whoa, what's this?" she put her coffeepot down to hold up a strange drawing of a tree.

Matt knew this one because David had drawn it earlier and explained that this tree represented the fragility of many fast-growing businesses. "Millions of people now join social networks at a speed previously unknown to man, not to mention all these transactions, and now billions of words and ideas are being sent around the globe at the speed of light. Over two hundred years of video viewing are uploaded to *YouTube* each month, for crying out loud! We've never experienced this before. It's completely changing the transfer of information. The younger now teach the older...."

Rose threw in her two cents, "And we oldsters begin to wonder what planet we're living on."

Steve added, "Tech tools and consumer goods promising convenience burst onto the scene, change our way of life, the way we work, and the very nature of socialization...and then, six months later, it's all outdated. It's hard to fathom."

Matt asserted, "You're whining, but you're right. Both the financial world and tech industries have had their share of rapidly growing glass trees, trees without any evidence of annual growth rings. Technology has permitted the growth at rates of speed that were, until only a short time ago, unimaginable."

John took the picture back from Rose and passed it over to Troy. "I don't think that growth in revenue or profits alone is a sufficient measure of success if it fails to measure qualitative growth. People need to grow both in skills for the future and personally. Customers should also be better off because of improved products and service."

Matt grunted, "It's good to be the Philosopher Accountant King. I like that."

Rose rolled her eyes at this new conversational direction. "I'm leaving you guys; I don't need to hear more of this."

Troy pointed at the roots of the tree, before tossing the sketch back onto the table. "Does this growth contribute any happiness or dignity to the lives of those it affects?"

John nodded again, "And you have the financial sector offering products that grow at parabolic rates and then implode. These products are designed for fast profits, not long-term growth. No thought of the qualitative side – no time to develop the employee, nor any consideration for the customers who are left holding the bag."

"Employees are at the core of every company and are its most valuable assets. But how many companies and organizations act like they believe that?" David added. "If these people – this core – are not developed and strengthened, then the prospects for such an entity remain fragile."

John continued, "Certain financial products – for instance, the credit default swaps – resembled these fast-growing crystal trees. This product added fuel to the real estate boom, which collapsed, devastating the lives of millions of people. These 'trees' simply had no substance. Mortgages were packaged in fragile glass, and, when the market tanked, there was no way to keep it from shattering. In hindsight, this fiasco was all about fast growth for a fast buck, and there we have it: a crystal tree."

Troy commented, "There's a tendency to measure the importance of things by their size: the size of the house, the size of the boat, the size of the stock portfolio, and the size of the profit it generates. But more doesn't necessarily mean better.

"Think for a moment about the beauty of a single rose." He pulled a drawing out from David's pile of sketches. His fingers touched the petals, and seemed to catch the droplets of water beading on the rose's surface. "It starts out as a small rosebud, but if we have just a little patience, we can watch it bloom into magnificence."

Rose

He clarified, "I'm not saying growth isn't important; it's an essential part of life. But it's the good that growth brings that matters. Growth for growth's sake has no lasting value."

John spoke up, "I once heard a preacher turned businessman, who led a Fortune 500 company, speaking about living growth. In his early days, he was task-oriented; he confessed that he saw people as a means to get work done. He viewed work as the end. Then he realized that he was reversing the positions of means and ends. He openly shared how his faith gave him the motive and power to change the way he viewed and treated other people. He said it wasn't easy, but that he was committed to helping people develop rather than to use people to accomplish the work as the end. What he said made sense to me."

Steve concluded, "Everywhere I go in the world I see our powerful brands displayed in neon lights. I also see evidence of our film, music, and dress entrenched in cultures around the world. All that we have exported is a manifestation of the success of our economic vitality. But what if the Tower challenges our culture and values? How will we defend ourselves? If that time comes, we will have to rely on what is on the inside – the strength of our character and strong values. When we are tested and challenged by the New World Order, we will know for sure whether our exceptionalism as a nation is solely directed at our economic vitality, or does it translate into the character of our people to defend our freedoms and our values?"

THE LAST TOWER

CHAPTER
09

THE UNIQUENESS
OF MAN

OHN MOVED THE COFFEEPOT ROSE had left behind to a safer spot on the table and straightened the stack of pictures. "Yeah, what happens when the Tower actually starts telling us what we can say and how to interact with people?"

"What conspiracy yarn are you spinning now?" asked Matt.

"It's no yarn, it's the truth. I just had a discussion with our HR director, and he was telling me about how more and more regulations are being added as to what we can say in the workplace to each other. It's like society tells us to 'run like the wind to your clean, comfortable homes and don't get involved.'"

Steve jumped in, "Maybe this is where we're going. Big Brother, the Tower, says, 'Leave it to us! Mind your own business. We'll take care of the people.'"

Matt asked, "So now you're saying the Tower is telling us not to be human?"

David replied, "If this Tower were to tell us that we should not be getting involved, should not mention God to a lonely troubled soul in the workplace, to me, that's the same as saying don't be human."

Troy reached over to refill John's coffee cup and then his own. He spoke slowly, as he looked down at his hands on the table rather than at any of the other guys. "People need to differentiate between the religion and the relationship. Too often, Christians are getting labeled as obnoxious, homophobic elitists, rather than examples of a loving God. The Apostle Paul wrote that even if we had faith to do things like move mountains, if we don't have honest love in our hearts for others, then we are nothing."

"You have to have a conscience to know you should love people, right?" asked John. "And here's the thing, thousands of years into the history of humanity, we still don't really know much about how our conscience works or how it fails to work, do we? Couldn't it be worn down or 'reprogrammed,' so that it wouldn't ring the warning bell anymore?"

"You're right," David answered, "the conscience can be worn down, but it can also be revived through pain and suffering. We have a heart. We need to feel other people's pain – if we don't, we're no better than machines."

Troy responded, "The conscience is one of our first lines of defense."

"Defense? Defense against what?" asked Matt.

"Well, think about it. We are constantly bombarded by all sorts of messages: how to achieve success, how to be happy, how to find fulfillment. All these messages assume that we are not at peace with ourselves. Many of these messages advise us on how we should think about all the flashpoints in the culture wars today. We are constantly called upon to make decisions and choices. If we lack a conscience sufficiently attuned to the truth, how can we detect a lie? Who's to decide which standard can serve as 'the truth'? And for that matter, just what is the truth? Isn't it all just relative? Plenty of people have died defending someone else's vision."

Matt offered, "I think the key questions here are... Is anyone getting hurt, are legal adults making the choices, and is 'the greater good of society' being served?"

After considering these questions, Troy responded, "We all know that wars have hurt many people, even if they began with good intentions. Prior to World War II, many Germans viewed Hitler as a hero. His vision pulled them out of the Depression and for a brief moment gave them back their dignity, but tragically this all ended in genocide and mass murder across Europe. His vision was clearly not the truth, yet the majority followed him blindly – a legacy of shame. History has proven that the Nazi's 'truth' was nothing but a 'big lie.'

"Now on to this business of adults making decisions – dare we mention baby seals and human beings in the same sentence? Take a breath in; say one thing. Blow it out; say another. This matter of conscience is more complicated than we originally thought.

And about this question of the 'greater good of society.' If you recall, long after England abolished slavery in 1833, this practice still continued in the United States. Whose good was served? Quite often 'natural law' runs counter to the common wisdom of the day. If history has proven anything, it's shown that 'society's conscience' can't be trusted. No country on earth is without a legacy of national shame, despite certain redeeming qualities."

John nodded his head, "Troy, I couldn't agree with you more, and if we don't do something here and now, history is likely to repeat itself."

Steve mused, "Not to jump from your historical timeline there, but I wonder if Groupthink – the conformity rules thing – might decide to take the place of parents' freedom to raise their children, particularly in the respective areas of morals and religious beliefs. Would the New World Order dare to tell parents that they must teach their children according to its precepts? How far might a government intrude into the family unit?"

Troy nodded his head and gestured, "What you say about parents is very significant. The relationship of a parent to a child is a natural relationship and not easily broken. The New World Order might very well try to neutralize the family's preeminence and make the Tower the father figure for society. This would be essential to have power over society and to transform it to its own image. Break up the family and you have dealt a fatal blow to society, as we know it. Better pray that we man-up with a big-time reality check before that happens. That would pretty much unravel everything as far as I'm concerned."

"Well, here's what we *do* know," added David. "Parents are the key influence in the development of the child's conscience and play an essential role in developing the whole emotional structure of what makes a human being tick. Fact is, too many

Corporate oak

parents are abdicating this responsibility so they can do something 'important' at work or in a ministry, or even because of a crazy obsession over a hobby or sport."

Steve interjected, "Now, I wouldn't say my dad was exactly hung up on sports, but he was a tough guy. I remember when I was a kid he used to accept all comers who challenged him to arm wrestling. Of course, he always won. Well, I guess you can figure where this is leading. One day, after I got home from active duty, I was sitting on the back porch with Dad and I challenged him to arm wrestle with me. Well, I beat him. Immediately, I challenged him a second time, proceeded to lose, and never challenged him again. Ya' know – you just don't want your dad to lose."

Troy grinned in agreement. "Guys like me... you know, from the lower Third Wheel – employed as window washers – we're really not 'down below.' We're right up there with the Big Boys at the penthouse level. We're told not to look and stare through the windows, but you can't help catching a glance now and then.

"So, one day, I was cleaning the windows on the top floor of an unusual office building. This place was designed to kinda resemble an oak tree – weird, but true. You see, the company president, the owner of this office building, admired the oak tree as a symbol of strength and trust. It reflected the president's own character as well.

"This highly respected man was regarded as a father figure by many of his employees. He always encouraged them to reflect on what really mattered in life, but never instructed them in their personal beliefs. He's the type of leader who would fight the managers of the New World Order for his workers' rights to speak freely about God.

"Anyway, there I was on the top floor, about to squeegee the window, when I happened to glance through the window and recognized it as the president's office. There he was holding his head in his hands, obviously troubled about something. He remained motionless the whole time I was washing the window. Well, I went on about the rest of my day.

"But I had to return for the night shift. That's when we clean the inside of the windows, when the staff has gone home. As as I was driving up to the building, I noticed that the top floor was still lit up. I wondered who in the world would still be in the president's office that late at night, but figured it must be him.

"So I made my way to the executive suite and sure enough the president was still seated at his desk. Poor guy seemed oblivious to any distractions. He only took notice of me when I said, 'Good evening.' At first, he seemed startled and distressed, but then relaxed when he recognized me.

"When he asked me why I was there, I told him that I had come to clean the interior surface of the windows, but while at work earlier in the day, I had noticed him through the window, and that he had appeared pretty disheartened. I was concerned for him. So, when I returned to work for my night shift, and saw that the lights were still on, I decided to come up to see if he was all right.

"Thanking me for my concern, he slowly began to open up. It was obvious that something was really bothering him.

I slowly coaxed his story out of him. He had loved his father, and in return had sought his dad's love and approval. I guess this guy was a great leader, too, and work took up all of his time.

"He had rarely received any attention from his father. So one day, when he was a child, to his great surprise his dad suggested that they go on a fishing trip. His eyes shone as he told me that he could still remember to this day how much it meant to him – to spend the whole day with his father.

"But then his demeanor changed. He had recently received a phone call with the sad news that his father's heart was failing, and he needed to get home ASAP. So he rushed to his father's bedside, only to learn his dad could no longer speak at this point. However, he was absolutely certain he'd seen love and remorse in his father's eyes.

"Soon after his father's death, this president searched his parents' big estate home in an attempt to find the diary that he knew his father had kept. He wanted to see firsthand what his dad had written about that fishing trip. Eventually, he found the book and the entry that described the day.

"At this point, the poor guy just broke down – sobbing. He reached into his desk and pulled out a small journal, opened it, motioning me to take it from him – too upset to even read out loud. So I took it and read the devastating words myself, 'A day wasted!' I couldn't believe my eyes!"

Troy stopped for a breath, and the men didn't move. "Well... after I got myself together, I assured him that he had a Father above who loves him in an everlasting way, and desires to spend every day with him!"

Fishing trip

Matt interrupted, "Okay, this is definitely one of the best stories you've ever told during my short life with you, but you *didn't* actually say that to him at that moment, did you?"

Troy just stared at Matt without answering. The other guys looked at each other around the table. And then they noticed that David's eyes were moist.

He awkwardly cleared this throat. "Guys, do you realize it's past 10 o'clock? Anybody want to call it quits for the night?"

Nobody moved, and Steve observed, "Well, it looks like nobody's in a hurry, but I could use a break." The others agreed to that.

When David got back to the table, he spoke with soft clarity. "Sorry for getting so weepy there, but the image of my own father, who just recently passed, is still fresh in my memory.

"He will always be the single greatest earthly influence on my life and my thoughts. No Tower...no government, no matter how great, would ever hold a candle to my dad's influence on me."

"What??" "Whoa!" "What are you talking about?" Chorused from around the table.

"You know my story." He held out the sketch that he'd just drawn. "I could have been this man. I thank God every day that I had the relationship with my dad that I had."

He looked down at the father reading his newspaper. "My dad had his wake-up call a few years after I graduated from college. He came to me and asked for my forgiveness and asked if we could start again. He told me how much he realized that he wanted to be there for me and that he realized how many opportunities he had missed in the past."

Treetop lookout

As he put down his sketchpad again, he said, "These days, the mere mention of anyone else's father just about brings me to tears."

Consoling his friend, Steve said, "Nothin' wrong with a few tears, man, believe me. If a man cries over something that matters, who cares what people think?"

"Yeah, so no more crying over rec league softball, okay?" Matt joked to offset the somber turn the conversation had taken. He paused and then asked with genuine interest, "Seriously, what was it like to re-establish a relationship with someone who'd been so distant for so much of your life?"

"It was a lot of work. He pulled back from his manic schedule and purposefully put me into his plans. I just loved to be alone with Dad.

"To give himself a quiet place for reflection, he built a special forest retreat. It was a lookout situated high above the rest of the trees. He would often take me to his refuge, and from that spot, we would look out across the treetops." David laughed, "I felt like I could see the whole world from up there. The whole forest took on an atmosphere of peaceful order, ya' know?

"I will never forget his words as he held my first child, 'Son, set your eyes on the things that last for eternity, and then shape your objectives around them.'"

CHAPTER
10

BREAD AND
CIRCUSES

Tower advertising

"SHAPE YOUR OBJECTIVES AROUND THE things that last for eternity," Troy murmured. Teenagers at a table across the room suddenly broke out in raucous laughter. Waitresses moved in to calm the roughhousing. "It must be hard," Troy said, "for a lot of young people today – especially since music and movies constantly encourage them to rebel against any authority – no father figure, no church influence, no thought of God."

"There ya' go," Matt suggested in feigned sincerity. "This New World Order just has to provide a variety of entertainment to win these young people over to them."

Steve jumped in, "Hey, didn't you say Caesar used bread and circuses to control the people? Weren't those circuses brutal and bloody – with lots of cheering and laughter as the 'contestants' hacked each other to pieces?

"Just imagine what some people might be willing to do to consolidate power into this Virtual Tower. It would be like Caesar's power projected around the entire world. Yeah, I think a lot of people would be willing to do all sorts of crazy things to achieve that kind of power."

"Two things are certain," declared Troy, "first, the managers of the Tower would try to eliminate any kind of threat to their power. Second, they would appoint themselves the 'Masters of Ceremony' to their own circus."

Matt gestured at the *Free Neighborhood News* in the stand by the diner exit, "Next, you're going to complain that this Tower would use advertising to draw people to the circus. You're going to go into DEFCON 6 conspiracy mode and say your Tower would even subvert the press."

David's eyes lit up. "Tell you what," he said as he turned to a fresh sheet of paper, "let's let our imaginations run with this. The circus would be an integral part of the Tower – a necessary distraction – a control mechanism. What sort of distractions might this New World Order use?"

He started to sketch as Steve's voice grew dramatic. "The first volley has got to be to grab attention. The Tower could get away with anything as news – sports, government, science, politics, and art – all aired as entertainment.

"Inconvenient truths would be simply edited or outright ignored. Thrilling disaster and war coverage would provide readers with shock and awe. Tragedies wrapped up with a music video would be narrated by glamorous women accompanied by dashing male counterparts. And don't forget the voyeurism... Everybody would know everybody else's secrets – all the lurid details."

John faked a pensive facial expression, "I'm sorry, when did we start talking about the current state of broadcast news?" The guys chuckled.

Steve agreed, "I'm so tired of the constant politicizing at all levels... Broadcasters and politicians don't seem to miss an opportunity to grandstand regardless of the nature of any tragedy."

John got David's attention and pointed to his sketchbook, "Sketch me a picture of a giant man tossing dice.

"That's it. Now, draw little human figures on the twelve faces of the dice." Pointing to David's newly sketched picture, John addressed the rest of the guys. "I want you to imagine a sideshow on the Ivory Tower level. The dice are used for gambling – this giant risks everything, but it's the 'little people' who take the fall."

This picture took Matt back to his daughter's situation. "It's the powerful people who roll these dice, and unfortunately, lots of people get hurt. Some game, huh? But it's entertaining to read about these giants-among-men, to hear of their exploits; it's the stuff of business legends."

John nodded, "I can just see these self-glorified managers of the Tower. People would fear their global power, and some would even regard them as immortal. The more the people feared these mighty men, the greater would be their belief in the Tower's power. The giant continues to roll the dice and gambles daily with the lives of customers, employees and their families, and entire communities. With each roll of the dice,

The colossus

he makes decisions affecting vast numbers of people, most of whom he has never set eyes on. As individuals, they are as far from his mind as east is from west."

Rose came up to the booth in her hat and coat. "Wilma's taking care of you for the rest of the night. But I warn you: I expect a mega tip tonight. Not only for serving you – but for having to put up with your wild stories; this Tower thing really spooks me."

They laughingly chorused their good nights as she headed out the door.

Matt doggedly returned to the 'circus.' "Hey, what about those phony guys on TV – those religious pickpockets? I call them 'Pocket Farmers.' They go after the poor, the infirm, and the downhearted. I'll bet more than one of them lies awake at night scheming how to separate good people from their wallets."

Troy readily conceded Matt's point, "You're right. I am so ashamed of these people. 'Pocket Farmers' fits 'em all right – they continually abuse this metaphor of sowing seeds. The only seeds these charlatans sow are those destined to end up in their own pockets. But the Bible has something to say about these people. Micah 3:11 talks about the rulers who governed for the bribes they got, the priests who taught God's laws only for a price, and the prophets who wouldn't prophesy unless they were paid. And then they went around claiming that because the Lord was with the nation, they were fine; there would be no consequences. Guys, God is infinitely more patient than any of us, but He will not be mocked. He'll have the final word."

Throne

Steve agreed, "Sounds like we're talking about Tetzel, the monk from Martin Luther's day who specialized in selling indulgences, assuring the poor and unsuspecting that money would get them out of purgatory."

"What Troy's saying is true," David acknowledged, "but I don't label everyone who uses God's name a 'phony.' Don't forget, even if the Pocket Farmers' motives are wrong, the victims are sincere, and God answers prayers in spite of the charlatans. And remember all the good people who quietly and selflessly serve in communities around the world. Many of them have given their lives for others, and they are good stewards. They don't twist the Bible to make a buck."

Troy concluded, "That said, at the end of the day, a New World Order would have to keep the general public distracted and controlled in order to keep people's minds from focusing on the Transcendent – the great 'I Am.' They'd probably have their own team of pseudo-religious charlatans, who, while outlawing all other voices, would concoct some notion about public safety. You know, the need to protect society from radical fanaticism, intolerance, and dogmatic hate speech or something like that. Of course, would this mean they would have to take that ultimate, and I might add *giant*, step over the line, the act of placing a man on the throne as a god?" Troy's sober prediction momentarily silenced all those seated around the table. Everyone felt a little uncomfortable.

"Once again," Matt responded wearily, "I respectfully disagree with you, but I'm too tired to argue at this point..."

"Yes, probably time to call it a night, day, *and* a discussion... Whatever, I gotta go home," added John. The others nodded in tired agreement. The discussion was going a bit random. It was time to end the session.

THE RED WAVE

THE LAST TOWER

CHAPTER
11

Back at the Diner

I**T WASN'T MANY WEEKS LATER** and David was the only one in the booth. It was raining again, and none of the gang was coming, so he had the whole table to himself and his sketchpad.

There were still a few more images that he could not get out of his mind: an empty throne, a giant wave, and an asylum cell. He smiled thinking about the razzing he would get for even mentioning these seemingly disconnected pictures in the same sentence. And, of course, he had already started sketching them.

He pulled out the worn leather satchel that held his art-work. Fishing inside, he had to pull out almost his complete collection of 'tower sketches' before he found the drawings that he wanted.

The idea of a waiting, empty throne had been an image that intrigued him. The Tower would definitely have a throne in it, and there would be those who would do everything they could to sit there. Nothing earth-shattering about that, people had pursued thrones for centuries. But who would sit on *this* throne in the Tower? Who would be put there? How much control would people allow this person – this power – to have over their hearts, minds, and wallets? And just how far would that entity go to completely rule everything? Yes, it definitely had some ominous mystery to it.

The throne was about the future, but this next image was about the here and now. His original idea had been to draw an actual ocean tsunami wave coming in for its cataclysmic landing upon a crowd of people standing in helpless terror before it. Nah, too cliché. Nevertheless, he had decided to stick with the cliché idea of the wave because it actually worked, but with one alteration...he had made it a wave of red ink about to devour a couple of innocent kids, a boy and a little girl, standing inside the false safety of a glass tower. Oh, he could already hear Matt snickering and making smart-aleck comments about his gloom and doom mindset. Undeterred, he put the finishing touches on some of the red highlights.

As he sipped some of his heavily creamed coffee, he looked over his last drawing. Neither the tsunami nor this next subject offered much hope, and he knew there had to be hope. An insane asylum was the perfect place to find it.

His eyes began to moisten a bit as he looked at a rather odd drawing of an insane asylum cell that he had been working on earlier. The style didn't quite fit the rest of the collection, but it was actually a pretty good drawing he thought. It was just an institutional small room with a cast-iron bed, and on the wall next to that bed were the scribbled words of an old hymn he could not quit humming and singing. The image was actually based on a true story about how the lyrics were discovered. He still found it difficult to believe someone in an insane asylum wrote them. It was an interesting narrative.

The story went that there was once an anonymous inmate at the asylum who after passing some time there, subsequently died. As his body was about to be removed from the room, someone noticed that these words had been inscribed on the wall in pencil. David thought they were quite possibly the most beautiful words he'd ever heard.

> Could we with ink the ocean fill,
> And were the skies of parchment made,
> Were every stalk on earth a quill,
> And every man a scribe by trade;
> To write the love of God above
> Would drain the ocean dry;
> Nor could the scroll contain the whole,
> Though stretched from sky to sky.

David's mental solitude was gently interrupted by his realization of someone's presence beside the booth. A little girl, who might have been all of seven, was standing wide-eyed looking at him and all the drawings.

"Are you a real artist?" she asked in childlike wonder.

"Well, I try to be," he laughed.

"Wow," she marveled, "are all of these pictures for a storybook or something?"

"I'd like it to be a book someday," David modestly answered.

"When I grow up I want to be an artist...after I swim at the Olympics," she added, not taking her eyes off all the drawings.

Red wave of debt

"What's your name, honey?"

"My name is Hope."

David smiled, "I love your name. That's beautiful!"

Oblivious to his compliment, Hope carefully touched the bottom corner of the last tower drawing that had ended up on the top of the pile when he had picked out the asylum sketch. Her freshly manicured little fingers, complete with tiny flowers, cautiously pulled the drawing closer to the edge of the table.

"Is this a true story or just make-believe?" she asked in complete innocence.

David paused for a few seconds as he stared down at the image and then into her big brown eyes.

"I'm not sure, sweetie. But I think we're about to find out..."

- The End -

Why do the nations rage and the peoples plot in vain? The kings of the earth set themselves, and the rulers take counsel together, against the Lord and against his Anointed, saying, "Let us burst their bonds apart and cast away their cords from us." He who sits in the heavens laughs; the Lord holds them in derision. Then he will speak to them in his wrath, and terrify them in his fury, saying, "As for me, I have set my King on Zion, my holy hill."

Psalm 2:1-6

FTER SEEING A SERIES OF articles on *"What's Wrong with the World?"* the Christian philosopher G.K. Chesterton sent a short letter to the editor.

"Dear Sir:
I am.
Yours truly,
G. K. Chesterton."

How would we respond to the same question? I believe the greatest threat to our future is a fearful or apathetic mind.

Let us consider our role and contribution in this rapidly changing world.

I leave you with the following questions and pictures to prompt careful thought and action.

WHAT ARE WE BUILDING,
AND FOR WHOSE BENEFIT?

HISTORY SPEAKS:
WILL WE LISTEN?

DOES THE SHADOW OF
THE TOWER CROSS YOUR PATH?

WILL WE PURSUE TRUTH
WHEREVER IT LEADS?